A Boat Named

MW01179019

Written by Doreen Dahl   Illustrated by Trevor Feierabend

A Boat Named Buttercup
Copyright © 2016 by Doreen Dahl

First printing September 2016

You may purchase this book by contacting Doreen Dahl at dorydahl@gmail.com.

To my son, Dan
Who fished the little yellow boat
called the Buttercup when he was young.
He has been my inspiration for this story.

Once upon a time there was a young boy named Danny who lived in a little fishing village in Alaska. Most of the fishermen had their own boats called gillnetters. They painted them black or gray or white.

Every day Danny would go out on the Valiant Maid with his father, Cap'n Ed, and his crew, Butch and Buddy, to help him catch fish.

One day Danny said "Mother, I want to buy my own boat to go fishing." His mother looked down at him and replied, "But you are so young!"

"But Mother, I have been saving all the money I made fishing with Father." he said. "Besides, I know how to fish now and I will be very careful".

"Very well" said his mother. "But you must promise to paint it bright yellow so everyone can see you in case there is trouble. Here is a can of buttercup yellow paint I found in the shed."

Danny went to Cap'n Ed to see what he should do. Cap'n Ed smiled and told him, "You better do what your mother says!"

So Danny promised his mother and painted his little boat yellow and named it the Buttercup. Some of the other fishermen made fun of him because his boat was different.

"Who paints their boat yellow?" they laughed.

But Danny didn't care, because he was captain of his very own boat and he caught lots of fish. When he came into the harbor his boat was always full of fish.

Sometimes, he would put his net out close to the shore where the fish swam, but he was always careful not to get too close to the giant waves crashing on the beach. The fishermen called them "breakers" and they were very scary.

One day after all the fishermen had laid out their nets and had begun to fish, a thick sea of fog rolled in. It covered the boats like a big gray blanket and nothing looked familiar. Even the big red Coast Guard boat couldn't see all the boats.

Danny could feel the fog's dampness on his face. He quickly pulled in his net and started for the harbor. He couldn't see a thing but he heard some of the fishermen yelling as they drifted out of sight.

Danny steered the Buttercup carefully through the fog when suddenly her engine sputtered and then stopped. "Oh, no!" Danny said. "This is not good." He tried to fix it but discovered the battery was dead. He could hear the giant waves crash on the shore. They grew louder and louder as the Buttercup drifted closer and closer. If they got caught in those breakers the Buttercup would wreck on the beach.

Danny felt very alone and scared. "If only someone would see me and come help!" he thought.

Suddenly, out of the fog, a big white boat appeared. It was Cap'n Ed with his crew on the Valiant Maid.

"Here!" Butch and Buddy yelled. "Catch the line! We'll tow you away from those breakers."

So Buddy, who was bigger and stronger, tossed the line high into the air and Danny caught it and tied it tightly to the Buttercup.

Then he climbed aboard the Valiant Maid as Cap'n Ed towed the Buttercup safely away from the breakers and to the boat harbor.

The next day Danny helped Cap'n Ed mend his nets. "How did you know I was in trouble, Father?" he asked.

"Your boat is yellow, Son" Cap'n Ed replied. "I could see you through all the fog, and I saw you were too close to the breakers." He smiled at Danny. "Being buttercup yellow saved your life."

The other fishermen soon heard the story and they never laughed at him again for being different. Some of them even painted their boats yellow!

Doreen Dahl is a published author of Alaska adventure articles and freelance writer. This is her sixth childrens' book. She is an Alaskan pioneer whose children and grandchildren were born and raised there. Her books show the adventure, the wildlife and the people of Alaska in a way children can understand.

Trevor Feierabend: 25, Illustrator/animator. Trevor is the owner of Miscreant Studios out of southern, California. He graduated from R.C.C. Norco, for animation, 3D art, fine arts and was awarded for many achievements in the process. Now he spends his time as a personal chef, illustrator and the art director of Miscreant Studios. Trevor is best known for his detailed stylized, funny looking characters with a balance of realism.

47068329R00020

Made in the USA
Middletown, DE
04 June 2019